Little Red Riding Hood

retold by Diane Stortz

Fairy Tale Classics

LANDOLL
Ashland, Ohio 44805
© The Landoll Apple logo is a trademark owned by Landoll, Inc.
and is registered in the U.S. Patent and Trademark Office.

n a small village at the edge of a great forest lived a little girl and her mother. The girl had a red, velvet riding cloak with a hood that her grandmother had made for her. She looked so pretty in the cloak and wore it so often, that the villagers all called her Little Red Riding Hood.

One day, Little Red Riding Hood's mother said, "Take this basket of bread and butter to your grandmother's house for me. Your grandmother has not been feeling well and has not been able to cook for herself."

ow the grandmother's house was on the other side of the great forest. Little Red Riding Hood knew the way through the forest, for she went there often. She wasn't the least little bit afraid. But her mother knew that any forest could be dangerous. "Go quickly," she said. "Don't dawdle. And stay on the path."

"I will," said Little Red Riding Hood. And off she went, carrying the basket of bread and butter.

he had not gone far when she saw a wolf.

"Good morning, Mr. Wolf," said Little Red Riding Hood.

"Where are you going?" the wolf wanted to know. "And what do you have in that basket?"

"I am going to my grandmother's house," said Little Red Riding Hood. "I am taking her this bread and butter from my mother, because she has been sick."

ow the wolf hadn't eaten in several days. Bread and butter would make a tasty snack, thought the wolf, but what I really want to eat is a tasty little girl! And I have a plan.

"Since your grandmother has been sick and unable to get out, perhaps she would enjoy a bouquet of wildflowers as well as the food in your basket," suggested the wolf.

L ittle Red Riding Hood looked around. The forest was filled with wildflowers of all colors. "Why, that's a lovely idea, Mr. Wolf," said Little Red Riding Hood. "But my mother did tell me not to stray off the path..."

"Well," said the wolf, "I'm certain that if your mother had thought about a bouquet of wildflowers, she would have agreed to let you pick some. Why don't you start with those red ones over there?"

"All right," said Little Red Riding Hood, and she left the path through the forest to wander under the trees looking for flowers.

When the wolf raced down the path to the house where Little Red Riding Hood's grandmother lived, he caught his breath and knocked on the door.

"Who's there?" called the grandmother.

"It's Little Red Riding Hood," said the wolf in a high, squeaky voice. "I've brought you some bread and butter."

"Then lift the latch and come in, dear," said the grandmother. She was tucked into bed and did not want to get up. But when the door opened and the wolf walked in, she sat straight up and then fainted from fright.

The wolf was not interested in eating the old woman, only Little Red Riding Hood. So he rolled the grandmother under the bed. He put on her lacy nightcap and jumped into her bed, pulling the covers up to his chin. Then he waited for Little Red Riding Hood to arrive.

hen Little Red Riding Hood could not carry any more wildflowers, she found the path and went on her way to her grandmother's house. She knocked at the door.

"Who is it?" called the wolf in his best grandmother voice.

"It's Little Red Riding Hood," answered the girl. "I've brought you some bread and butter and a bouquet of wildflowers."

"Lift the latch and come right in, dear," said the wolf.

ittle Red Riding Hood went inside.
"Come closer, my dear," said the
wolf. Little Red Riding Hood went closer,
but not too close.

"My goodness, Grandmother," she said.
"What big eyes you have!"

"The better to see you with, my dear," said
the wolf.

"And what big teeth you have,
Grandmother," said Little Red Riding
Hood.

he better to eat you with!" cried the wolf. He sprang out of bed and tried to grab the little girl, but she was too quick for him. She dropped her basket and ran out the door.

A hunter who was passing through the forest saw Little Red Riding Hood run outside with the wolf close behind her. The hunter chased the wolf deep into the forest. When the hunter came back, he went inside with Little Red Riding Hood to help her look for her grandmother. They found her standing beside her bed, looking quite shaken.

he danger is over now," said the hunter.

"The hunter chased the wolf away!" cried Little Red Riding Hood.

"Thank you for saving Little Red Riding Hood, sir," Grandmother said to the hunter. "Please stay and join us for tea."

So the hunter sat down with Little Red Riding Hood, and her grandmother and drank tea and ate bread and butter. And although the bouquet of wildflowers made a lovely centerpiece, Little Red Riding Hood never strayed off the path in the forest again.